Clint Faraday
book thirty nine
A Grave Mistake

Clint and Tyna are having a meal in La Tipica when a woman at a near table makes a number of loud com-plaints about the people at a close table and about the Indios and about Panamanians in general.

Considering who the people were at the close table, Tyna says she's making a grave mistake to be denigrating those people.

She didn't mean "grave" the way it turned out.

Contents

About the author

CD Moulton has traveled extensively over much of the world both in the music business, where he was a rock guitarist, songwriter and arranger and in an import/export business. He has been everything from a bar owner to auto salvage (junkyard) manager, longshoreman to high steel worker, orchid grower to landscaper, tropical fish farmer to commercial fisherman. He started writing books in 1983 and has published more than 350 books as of January 1, 2023. His most popular books to date are about research with orchids, though much of his science fiction and fantasy work has proven popular. He wrote the CD Grimes, PI series, and the Det. Nick Storie series, Clint Faraday series, and many other works.

He now resides in Gualaca, Chiriqui, Panamá, where he writes books, plays music with friends, does research with orchids and medicinal plants. He has lately become involved in fighting for the rights of the indigenous people, who are among his closest friends, and in fighting the extreme corruption in the courts and police in Panamá.

He offers the free e-book, *Fading Paradise*, that explains what he has been through because of the corruption.

CD is the discoverer of the Chadam Protocol for curing cancer.

Facebook page Ambrosia peruviana for cancer.

A Grave Mistake

A Disturbed Meal

"I love the shrimp here!" Tyna, wife of Clint Faraday, retired PI from Florida, USA, said, as they were having a delicious shrimp dinner at La Tipica. "I'm glad you eat so much. It's always more than I can hold.

"This would be almost perfect if it weren't for that loud-mouthed obnoxious gringa."

She was referring to a woman at a table next to them who was complaining in denigrating words about everything that came up. There were two woman at the table, one who was very quiet and obviously embarrassed by the antics of this one. They were both more than attractive except for the opposed personalities. The loud one was a very controlling type, the other a meek mouse type.

"... I mean, the food is good and there's plenty of it, but the service is awful! We don't even get bread? They put *catsup* on the table?

"Where is your boyfriend when we need him? He may be a gigolo who only uses you to be near me, but he's better than what we have here!

"I'm not used to this! I dine where there is some pretense of class!"

"Pretense is about as far as she'd ever know," Tyna remarked, just loud enough for her to hear. The mousy one almost giggled. The loud one turned to stare at Tyna.

"Who do you think you are to say such a thing about anyone? You're just an Indian who never knew the finer things in life and who never will!"

Clint stood and went to the table.

"If you say one more word about my wife I'll probably lose my temper," he said quietly. "If you don't like things here you can always go back to whichever trailer park you came from in Podunk Arkansas!

"Learn to conduct yourself in a civilized manner or refrain from frequenting places where people who do have some class go!

"For your information, they don't usually serve bread with meals here unless you request it. Catsup is put on the table for gringos because they'll usually ask for it. This isn't the US. The customs are different."

"I ... you...! You can't talk to me like that! I'll have you arrested!"

"Ilene! Shut up, please! You're making a fool of yourself! No one here cares that you wrote a book! They don't even read English!

"I'm sorry, Sir. My sister has let a bit of success go to her head I'm afraid."

"Well, they should learn English if they want people to come here and spend their money!"

"She wrote a romance novel that's gotten a lot of promotion and is selling very well," the sister said. "No one here knows that she's a famous author or they'd probably kow-tow to her like they do back home."

"She wrote a book? How nice," Tyna, who had come to the table said. "One comes *to* spend their money, not *and* spend their money. That's a split infinitive, you see. I'd think an author would know that."

"Actually, she's written three. This last one is selling well, so the other two are also selling. Writer's are strange people, you'll find."

"I have to agree with that, though not so many in this way," Clint said.

"I'm right here! You could include me in the conversation at least. You could show a person a little respect!" Ilene snapped. "Joyce, these people bore me! Get rid of them!"

"We're already showing you as little respect as possible under the circumstances," Tyna replied sweetly. "I realize it's more than you deserve, but that's how it goes.

"So you wrote a book! Big deal! The man who was with us earlier writes books. He's a weird character, but he's not obnoxious with it."

"I suppose his book's all about snakes and crocodiles in the jungle, just like ten thousand others!" Ilene replied, haughtily.

"Probably some of that. I can't conceive of anyone who writes a romance novel saying some other kind of work is like ten thousand others in that tone. A romance novel is more like ten million others.

"Mi amor, how many books has Dave had published? Do you know?" Tyna asked, in her sweet voice.

"Something over a hundred fifty. I think it was one sixty three the other day when he uploaded that *Inverted Paradise* thing. It's a romance in a way, but a bisexual one."

"He writes *porno*?!" Ilene asked, shocked.

"Definitely not. It's erotic to an extent, but he doesn't write pornography like so many of those romance things," Tyna replied.

"It's bisexual?" Joyce asked, interested.

"Yes," Clint answered. "It's sort of the normal state among a lot of people here.

"We'll leave you to your meal. Please don't disturb others with your complaints."

"I'll try to shut her up," Joyce promised with a grin Ilene couldn't see. Clint and Tyna went back to finish their meal as six men were escorted to the table to the other side of Ilene and Joyce. Things were quiet for a few minutes, then "My dear god! We're in some kind of mafia hangout! We're surrounded by thugs!" Ilene cried

"Ilene! Please shut up! You don't speak enough Spanish to know what you thought you heard was what you heard!"

"I know what assassinate means!"

"Ilene! Please!"

Clint went to them. "Assessinado means killed. It isn't the same as in English. It's killed by any number of things, even a car wreck.

"Sr. Morales and Sr. Quinteros are court judges. They're talking about cases in their courtrooms. You would do well to remember where you are. You obviously *don't* speak enough Spanish to know what you're hearing!"

"Thank you, Sir. She should learn to keep her big mouth shut before she gets us into serious trouble.

"I'm Joyce Carstairs. This is my sister, Ilene."

"Clint Faraday. My wife is Tyna."

"I think I've heard of you! You're a detective?" Joyce asked. "Then Dave is that one who writes detective novel series and science fiction and paranormal and everything else?"

"Yes.

"Joyce, try to get through to Ilene that she's a nobody here, just like everyone else. If she knew some of the people who come here she would be impressed, because she's the type to be impressed. They aren't. They won't be impressed by her book. There's an entirely different value system here."

"She's impressed by money. She never had any before. When you suggested we're trailer trash you came a lot closer than I want to admit.

"I read something in that *True Crime* or one of those magazines. You got six million dollars for one of your cases that you didn't even know was in your name? Hank says you have a lot of cases that pay in the millions."

Clint grinned and nodded. He went back to their table and they ordered dessert. Ilene was quieter. She was asking Joyce if she was serious that Faraday was worth six million dollars. Joyce had answered that was only one of the cases where he got millions. Hank said that there was a pirate treasure one where he got over a hundred million that he got ten percent of tax free or something. She was pouring it on.

Ilene did get a little loud about "those hoods, judges or not," at the next table.

"She's making a grave mistake talking about people like that in public," Tyna warned. "The two are judges. The four really are thugs. I hope none of them speak English."

"Two of them do, minimum. I've talked with them before. Not the judges."

They finished their meal and left.

Clint went out on the porch at the pensión early to find Joyce struggling to get a large maleta into a cab. Clint helped her. Ilene came out, dressed like those old safari movies. Joyce grinned and said they were going to go to that trail on the volcano to spend their day hiking to the summit. She was dressed in blue jeans and a flannel shirt, which she said was too hot for David, but they told her it was cold on the mountain. Clint said to take raincoats. This time of year the rains were almost every day. "Excuse me? You're hiking the mountain trail with that ridiculous bag?"

She laughed. "No, that's to be dropped off at the bookstore at Dolega on our way. She's going to have a book signing tomorrow."

"Here? You're kidding, right?"

"Kidding?"

"I doubt there are fifty people in the province who read romance novels. Thirty of them don't speak English."

"Really? That'll be great fun – for me!"

Ilene made it a point to avoid speaking to Clint. She asked Joyce where Hank was. Joyce said he went to Boquete to get away from her. They soon got in the cab and left. Jeff, the owner of the pensión, came out to say the day would probably be pleasant enough now that the pain in the ass was gone for a few hours.

"My god! You'd think she was the queen of Panamá the way she goes on! She really does think she's some kind of super star!

"You know those camera crew guys from the TV documentary they're making? Freddy and Gilda and George? They're in the cabin?

"She found out they're a TV camera crew. She was asking about camera angles and if she should use special makeup and was it true that she would have to lose weight. They asked her what the hell she was talking about and she said she was probably going to have to star in a movie about one of her books or something and needed the advice! She didn't have much experience with theater. Christ Almighty! Can you picture her in a movie? My god!"

"Yeah. Cinderella's sister. She's a load!"

"I feel a little sorry for Joyce. She's nice, in a sort of desperate way. She puts up with hell from her sister. She says the only experience Ilene has in the theater was in a silly high school play where she played a dingy bimbo, which was almost type-casting.

"I'm surprised Lloyd isn't going with them, but I can see why! Hank had the sense to get away from them."

"Hank?"

"Hank Little. I think he's gay. He's not really with them, but he and Joyce seem to be friends. Ilene pretends she doesn't like him, but she confides in him a lot."

"Lloyd?"

"Her agent or something. He's good at having appointments somewhere where she isn't. He's in there watching the news on TV. Come on. I'll introduce you. He's not so bad."

They went inside where Clint was introduced to Lloyd Baskins. They chatted a few minutes. They were talking about why they were in Panamá.

"Her stupid book," Lloyd replied. "She wrote a story about a young virgin who goes on a safari in South America with a group. She fell in love with the trailmaster and, as is perfectly natural in romance novels, treated him like secondhand dirt, so that he fell in love with her at the end and they lived happily ever after, roaming through the mountains of Panzuela."

"Panzuela?"

"She hadda call it somethin'!" They laughed.

"She's doing this bit so she can pretend she had a clue as to what she wrote. I don't think she has a clue about anything."

"She'd better learn not to run her mouth in public about people she doesn't know. She could get in serious trouble here if she pulls the crap she pulled in La Tipica last night with the wrong people."

"Joyce told me about that scene. Joyce is a sweet doormat for her. I'd feel sorry for her if that wasn't exactly what she needs, somehow. At first I was ready to defend her, but she makes excuses for it to go on and on. I don't get it, but it's a psychological type the same as Ilene's a psychological type."

He was toying with a paperback book on the table. It was *Jungle Nights, River Days* by LaVonne LeVogue.

"LaVonne LeVogue? Really?" Clint remarked.

Lloyd turned the book over to show a picture of Ilene laying on a couch with a come-hither look at the camera. Her hair was darker and the eyes were made up with a Spanish fireball look.

"She can be sexy as hell so long as she keeps her mouth shut. Illusions come crashing in with the first sentence."

Clint nodded. "And sister Joyce is much better looking and sexier. She works hard to hide it. It gives me a ... I think I see why she was interested in that."

"In what?"

"A friend writes books. He just published one I said could be a sort of romance novel, but of a different kind. It's a bisexual story."

"And Joyce was immediately interested?"

Clint nodded again.

"I don't think ... maybe she is a lesbian. She tries awfully hard to not get involved with any man. She doesn't date. Ilene does, but it's only for a date or two, though Joyce says she used to date a lot – before she became queen of the fair. The love scenes between the hero and ten other girls before he falls in love with a silly empty-headed virgin seem to have a lot of personal experience behind the descriptions."

"It gets into porno? She seemed shocked at the idea in Dave's books."

"No. It's erotic as hell, which is why she sells so many. She went back and revised the two she wrote before this one to have some such scenes. She goes to a point and lets you cross it in your own mind. 'She moaned as he moved against her and clung to his broad shoulders. The explosion was near!

"Next morning, she got out of the shower and looked at last night's perfection laying there in innocent beauty. A warm feeling moved from a point to encompass her being. She shuddered in pure delight and moved to turn on the coffee pot.' Pretty damned good, but she never crosses the line. Hitchcock was *the* master of that."

"Amen! So she writes about it, then wants to see how close she came?"

"Without the hero. She wouldn't want to share the stage."

Tyna came out with Nito, their two year old son, and Nicole, their four month old daughter. They went to breakfast

Clint came back from the shopping with Tyna and the kids to find Lloyd talking with two police officers. He knew them both and asked what was going on.

"A couple of the ladies on the hiking trail have wandered off somewhere and don't answer calls or anything they've tried," Esteban replied. "She works for or with Mr. Baskins here. We were informing him."

"Publicity stunt?" Clint asked Lloyd. "It won't work here, but it might get some attention in the states."

"I wouldn't put it past her for one tenth of a second, but I'm not involved. That kind of crap worked fifty years ago. That's about where she is.

"There is one thing that brings in doubts."

"Yeah. Picture her spending the night up in those mountains."

"Well, I hope they find her soon. I've had about enough of her. I can capitalize on having made her and make it pretty good from now on. She can keep me out of anything in the future, but my part of what's already done is solid. For six more years I get mine.

"To show you how concerned I am, what can you tell me about this La Esmeralda Club I keep hearing about?"

"It's the highest class whorehouse here."

"If I hadn't met your wife, I'd ask if you cared to try it out."

They talked about other things. The police left. Clint and Tyna packed the things they'd bought and were going to catch the early bus to Soloy. They went to a local restaurant where they had a delicious traditional meal. There were several families there with small children and one with a baby about Nicole's age who didn't stop her loud screaming and crying the whole time it was there. Clint could tell it was temper and not much else. Three children Nito's age were running wild around the place. The parents didn't make more than a halfhearted attempt to control them. One father swatted a little girl on the butt. She cried for ten seconds, then went back to being a little monster.

The waitress complimented Tyna about how well-behaved her children were.

"I would never embarrass my parents by acting like that!" Nito declared. "They like for me to be with them. If I acted like that they wouldn't want me here. It's so stupid!"

"We don't get many Indios here, but they never act up. The children. I don't understand it."

"You can't. It's the different way your were raised," Tyna replied. "My baby's are always touching me or Clint. When we have to be away for any time at all they're touching a relative or close friend. They're secure. We want and love them and they know it. Clint would never hit his children. How can they be secure when a parent hits them?"

"I wouldn't hit my children. They don't act like that. I'll cut off their allowance in a minute and they know it!"

"What's an allowance?" Nito asked.

"I give them each a dollar every week for things they want. Two if they're especially good."

"But why?"

"It's an allowance. It's part of ... you don't get an allowance?"

"I get some money whenever I need it when we sell vegetables or like that. What do they do for their allowance?"

"Do? It's an allowance."

"For nothing? It's so you can say they don't get it if they act like that?"

Clint could see this would get worse, so said, "Nito, this is a different culture. They don't raise vegetables or fish or have cows like we do. They have to work like this lovely lady to earn money for food and clothes."

"Weird! Where is their place if they get an allowance and don't do anything?"

"It's a different culture," Tyna replied. "It's why your father and I don't like cities. People spend their lives looking for a place to belong. We have one when we're born. We can't really understand them and they can't understand us.

"Well, Clint. He's lived in both cultures."

"It's because you don't have to have money like we do," the waitress said. "You would see things differently if you were around a money culture. You don't have much, but you don't need much."

"He's Clint Faraday," Tyna said. "If there's one thing he has a lot more of than he wants or needs it's money."

"The detective? I'm honored!"

"I'm just a guy who's found the place where he belongs. Have a good evening! Coin deo, as we say."

They left and went back to the pensión. Ilene and Joyce still hadn't been found.

He talked with Jeff a bit. Jeff didn't think it was any publicity stunt unless they had sneaked into Boquete or Volcan and were in some upper class hotel.

"She's staying here in a pensión, for Christ's sake! She doesn't get the service she would get in the Ciudad de David at a hundred fifty a night. It's just *not* what she's used to!"

"Joyce says you called her trailer trash. That's really what they are."

"Joyce isn't."

"No. Joyce is okay. If she just wasn't so needy, I could go for her."

Clint nodded.

In the morning Clint put his family on a private helicopter to be taken to their place in Quebrada Tula. Lloyd had approached him while he was having a coffee on the porch before sunrise and said he was finally worried. Nothing had been heard of about Ilene or Joyce. If it weren't for the signing that was to take place this morning, he wouldn't worry about them. Ilene wouldn't miss that opportunity to be the center of attention. Joyce was far too levelheaded to allow one of Ilene's fantasies to go this far. Tyna and family were used to this when the detective business came up.

Clint and Lloyd went to Cerro Punta to the start of the trail. They talked with the officer who was directing the search. Santos, the officer in charge, was a friend who had worked with Clint on a case. He said he'd spotted something that may mean something or may not. A place where two people or more had stayed near the trail. They had cut some branches in a small spot that would allow them to see the trail.

"I saw the little cut. It's about a third of a meter, but is obvious if you're looking for it. I went in to where I found a number of fresh cigarette butts laying around, some menthol and some regular.

"I had the men check the sides from below and above to find where anyone left the trail in that area. I felt that abductors would wish to remove them from the other hikers' sight as soon and as quietly as possible.

"It has been only half an hour or a little more. I am hoping something more will be found.

"Clint, I will say this to you, but to no one else. (Lloyd was a distance away, talking with another officer). A man from Rosario Generosa has told me we are not to look too hard for these women. He swears they will be back soon. They are being warned about making charges against ... people. They will say they wandered off the trail and got lost."

"I see. I think I know what it's got to be about. Joyce isn't the one they want to shut up. She won't talk anyhow."

There were calls for a medic and ambulance from a distance ahead. Santos made the call on the radio as they rushed to the voice. It was coming from a little ravine just off the trail. Clint, Lloyd and Santos climbed down through the rough stubbly scrub and rocks to find two officers administering to Joyce, who seemed to be unconscious. They helped hold brush away for two of the officers to carry her up to the trail as the ATV with a medic aboard screeched to a stop. They loaded her onto the stretcher. The medic said her signs were reasonably strong after a minute. They took her back to the waiting ambulance.

Clint and the officers and Lloyd climbed back down and went farther down the ravine, but didn't find anything more. They went back up to the trail for Santos to show Clint where the lookout cutting was. Santos thought, then headed up the trail a ways. He didn't find anything. Clint moved around the area and found what may have been another lookout point a short ways farther along.

Santos got a call on his cellular. He listened a moment and grunted. When Lloyd and the others were a little ahead he whispered to Clint, "She ran and fell. They did not push her. She was not meant to be hurt. He does not know where the sister is. The others came out without either of them."

They went on until they heard calls from back toward the trail start. It was on a little side trail that led to a small vale. There was a woman and two police officers there. The woman led them to a small flat sandbar in the lazy river where there was a mound. A hand was sticking out from the mound.

"I don't think Tyna meant this when she said Ilene'd made a grave mistake," Clint said sourly.

"What?"

"It's something that was said in a restaurant about Ilene Carstairs. Tyna said she'd made a grave mistake in challenging two judges and four thugs. That was a long way from smart."

They called in a crew to take pictures and do a CSI, then she was dug out. There was nothing to say how she'd died. Santos said the ME would determine cause of death. Clint and Lloyd went to the hospital to find a man Lloyd introduced as Hank Little, a close friend of Joyce and Ilene.

"Have they found Ilene yet? Is she alright?"

"No. They've found her. She's dead."

"Dead? Why ... what happened?

"We're trying to piece it together now," Clint replied. "It seems Joyce and Ilene were abducted. We think Joyce got away from them and ran, but fell into a ravine. It probably saved her life. Ilene didn't get away. Now she's dead."

"Do you have any idea ... they don't know she's a successful writer here. They weren't after ransom or anything. Why would they kidnap her? What was it for?"

"We don't know. She may have crossed paths with what passes for the mafia here," Lloyd said. "Joyce was telling me about the restaurant where you told her to shut up. I checked. Two were judges and four were gangsters. She probably saw them pass a bribe or something."

"That doesn't make sense," Clint argued. "I saw them. So did a number of other people in the restaurant. She made remarks that may have made someone want to teach her a lesson about respect or something, but they wouldn't kill her. They'd just scare the piss out of her."

"Maybe when Joyce ran they thought she'd died from that fall and knew they were in for it if Ilene was still alive and could testify against them," Lloyd said.

"It's thin, but a possibility," Clint replied. "I know the ways of the people she was talking about. Kidnaping her and scaring the holy living piss out of her would fit. If Joyce ran and fell into that ravine, they wouldn't worry about it. It would go before one of the judges they own and he'd rule that she wasn't pushed, she fell. No crime. Accidental death through misadventure. Next case.

"What's the matter?" Hank was shaking and obviously terrified.

"But...! Joyce will be able to identify them for killing Ilene! They aren't afraid of the law here if they can silence her before she can identify them! You've got to protect her!"

"She won't be harmed further," Clint promised. "I can see she's safe. I've had to protect people before."

"God! I hope so!"

They talked with the doctor. He said she was sedated. She had a minor, as those things go, skull fracture. She would be disoriented for awhile when she regained consciousness. It wouldn't be a good idea to rely on what she remembered until she had stabilized. About six hours.

Clint said he would have an officer posted to protect her. He knew someone involved in it and would have a little chat with him.

"A judge?" Hank asked.

"No. A gang boss."

Clint left them and went to the station to ask his friend and head of violent crimes where Rosario Generoso could be found. He got an address and phone number. He had to promise he wouldn't let Generoso know, ever, where he got the number. Generoso didn't know they had it.

"The one who reported to Santos on the trail?"

"To what and whither doest thou remonstrate thence and thusly?"

Clint grinned and gave him the old one-finger salute and went out.

The Victorio Gonzales Edificio. A big building that looked abandoned and falling apart from outside, but had two Mercedes and a Mazeratti sitting in the parking lot. Yeah, right!

Clint took out his cellular and called the number.

"Si? Quien habla?"

"I'm Clint Faraday. I need to speak with you. It's urgent."

"Ah! Mr. Faraday! I'd ask how you got this number that no more than six people know, but you are a very resourceful man! I will speak with you. Where shall we meet?"

"I'm right outside."

He laughed. "Could I ask how you know where and that I'm here?"

"Your Mazeratti is sitting right there in plain view."

He laughed again. "'When all else fails, look to the obvious.' That is a direct quote from one of your friend's books. Geraldo will meet you at the door." He rang off.

Clint went to the (apparently) rusty steel door and waited for half a minute until a big Mestizo came to lead him through a bunch of rubble to a sagging elevator door. Inside, the elevator was quiet and plush. They went to the fourth floor. The building had ten.

"Anybody'd think they'd be on top. Jefe's not stupid."

He went into a littered hallway and to a door with a dirty broken glass panel with cardboard tacked across the panel on the inside. Geraldo opened the door, waved Clint inside and went back down the hall.

It was as quietly plush as anyplace he'd ever been. A beautiful woman smiled warmly and said, "Mr. Faraday, if you will be so kind as to have a seat Mr. Generoso will be with you momentarily. He is with a business acquaintance at the moment. It will not be long.

"May I bring you coffee or tea? Something stronger?"

"I would appreciate strong coffee, black. Thank you."

She went into a small office and came out immediately with a steaming cup of very good coffee. "Mr. Generoso likes this grind. He says he is a coffee addict, joking, of course."

"I am too, but not joking. Many a truth is said in jest."

He sat with the coffee. She brought sticky buns, which Clint loved! He thought right then he was going to like Generoso, gangster or not!

After about five minutes Vasily Armakovich, a head man in the Russian Mafia, came out of the office, looked surprised, grinned, and said, "I should never be surprised by anything from you, but I am! How are you and the family, my friend?

"Rosario, I see you know my good friend, Clint! Why didn't you tell me?"

"We have never met. I have seen Mr. Faraday in places. We never spoke."

"You'll like him. No bullshit. Right on the table and here's the line. You don't cross it and there will never be any problem. I will guarantee my friend, Clint. He is the most rare kind of human being in today's sad world. He is honest. If he says a thing, it is written in titanium steel!

"Clint, I must go. Had I known I would see you I would have arranged to stay the night, but business – no remarks please! – is the harshest of taskmasters."

He hugged Clint, waved, threw the beautiful woman a kiss and left.

Rosario shook his head, shrugged, grinned and laughed. "He's a trip, as you gringo hippies say.

Come on in. I'll try not to be the formal criminal syndicate master.

"That's mostly pure bullshit, too. Almost all my businesses are legitimate."

"Almost?"

He laughed and gave Clint the finger. Clint grinned.

"There are times when one must fight fire with fire or he will be the one burned.

"What can I do for you, Clint?"

"I want to know what's going on with the Ilene Carstairs thing."

He nodded. "We did not do that. When we left her she was a bit ... disconcerted. The boys had explained a few of the facts of life. Her sister was allowed to run away. We did not know she had fallen. We would have taken her immediately to hospital.

"I swear to you she was left near where you found her. She was very frightened, but she was unharmed when my boys left her there. They say she was sitting on a rock and that she was defiant and thought they couldn't touch her. She also knew she couldn't touch my friends or myself."

"She wasn't a very nice person. Someone else had some reason to want her dead and used you as an excuse and cover. You're to be the goat, but they'll know you're untouchable.

"Why bother with some self-important piece like her anyway?"

"As you said, she was not a nice lady. She was into blackmail. Very heavily. She thought she could blackmail me. She was unsophisticated in the ways of another country.

"Clint, she thought because she took some candid pictures of myself and some others in a restaurant that she could blackmail me because I was even there with them. I think politics in the United States would make my meetings something sinister that would lose an election for me or something as silly.

"I do not like blackmailers. I would laugh at people for suggesting such a thing, but she was going to start a lot of trouble through the gringo newspapers and television.

"My boys explained to her that there are some things one never attempts should one care to live to be a ripe old age. One is, as they put it to her, trying to blackmail a mafia don who could order her and her family be wiped from the face of the Earth and forget he'd given the order the next day when he went to the golf club while her family was removed to the second cousin. They had pictures of some of those drug cartel killings. Very gory and very horrible. She got the point.

She claimed it was only a joke, that she would never actually *do* anything like that!"

"Uh-huh."

"Well, after that lecture I'm quite sure she wouldn't ever *do* anything like that."

"You have a point. All I wanted was your word you didn't actually *do* anything like that to her. I appreciate the rest. I already felt someone else was involved. You wouldn't knock over some obnoxious gringa for calling you a hood."

"After all, I *are* one!" They both laughed. Clint had been right. He did like Rosario Generoso, mob boss.

He still had to find a killer. That she was into blackmail gave him a good way to approach it.

He left Rosario awhile later and headed back to the station. Tonio said there was a report from the ME. She had died of an embolism in the brain. A vein had burst. She had been, literally, scared to death.

What next? That would be the end of it if she hadn't been crudely buried. Someone thought they'd killed her in a more ... not necessarily!

Time to drop back and regroup. This thing was suddenly coming from an unsuspected angle.

Okay. The mob was eliminated in his mind as being behind Ilene's death – even though more than a minor charge of incidental homicide would apply here. There had to be something else.

That left Lloyd, Hank, the judges, or the mob. Eeny, meeny, miny, mo.

He didn't suspect Joyce, though she may have been in league with someone else. He didn't really suspect the mob. Rosario was telling the truth.

The judges could have hired someone. They certainly knew who and where. He didn't really suspect them.

Lloyd? He somehow couldn't figure a motive except that she was a blackmailer and may have had something on him. He did say he had it made no matter what with her books.

Hank? He didn't know diddly about Hank. He seemed to be someone who hung around Ilene and Joyce, but there didn't seem to be a reason for that. He was fairly obviously gay or bi, with leanings toward the homosexual end. That didn't seem to offer motive for blackmail. You couldn't very well blackmail a person for something that was obvious and known.

That had to mean there was something or someone else he didn't know about. Any blackmailer, amateur or professional, would have "insurance" that the information would be made public if anything unpleasant were to happen to them. If she was blackmailing any of these it would be known soon enough.

He went to the station to ask that Tonio check up very carefully on those from the states. He said he was sure Rosario didn't have anything to do with it.

"She died of natural causes, probably hastened by someone, but they'll get away with it," Tonio cautioned. "Don't waste a lot of time with it."

"I know. I just wonder if this one thinks they can get away with eliminating anyone else who they decide they don't like."

Tonio thought and slowly nodded. He brought the computer terminal around and told Clint he was better at this kind of thing than he could ever be. Have a go!

Joyce Carstairs had almost nothing against her. She had been an average popular student in high school and had leaned toward the arts in talent.

She sang. She was very good on the flute. Her idol was Ian Anderson. She liked the rock type of music. She wrote some songs that were recorded by major garage bands. They were quite above average, but those things seldom went anywhere nationally without promotion, which she could never afford.

Ilene was a little more popular. She was runner-up for prom queen and such. She never seemed to quite have the talent for anything. She was an average student.

Interesting. She had been warned four times in two years about being in places where she was not allowed because of her age.

Not much. Henry "Hanky-panky" Little was popular among the arts group. He was a little bit wild at times. He never quite got into trouble, but there was always suspicion about "many things" was why the Hanky-panky moniker in the school yearbook. He was arrested once for contributing. He bought beer for several minors, but he was just seventeen, meaning they couldn't make that charge stick. The manager of a local bar was convicted of selling alcohol to minors and fined a thousand dollars and put on probation for one year.

Lloyd Baskins was talent agent for writers and musicians. He was moderately successful on the local scene and had recently gone national when a writer of romance novels got a near best seller published through his agency. He was never in trouble in a legal sense, but had been in trouble with women before. Several women had filed complaints with ASCAP and such that he had rules for using his services that were not the kind of thing that should be tolerated. It was a "casting couch" kind of deal. They wouldn't mind so much in today's world except he was too kinky in his demands.

That was what he had. He couldn't really add up much of anything from it. It may be the basis for Ilene blackmailing any or all of them.

That was a point to consider. Joyce wasn't so much the little mouse type when she wasn't with Ilene. Maybe Ilene was blackmailing her own sister.

This was a little beyond anything he'd done. He was determined that it wouldn't get away from him. He had to know, even if there wouldn't ever be prosecution. That was a part of his personality.

He sat back. Tonio asked what he'd learned.

"To tell the truth, I learned that they were all sort of stupid to let her blackmail them in the first place. I think it was all on silly things based on personal fears."

"What do you mean?"

"Lloyd used his position as agent to try to get female clients into kinky sexual situations. Hank bought beer for minors, but he was a minor so the bartender got fined. That kind of thing. Important and disgraceful in a small town, but a big 'Yawn! So what?' anywhere else. She tried the same kind of petty crap against Rosario and got slapped down. His boys put the fear of the drug cartel executions into her. That would serve as a reason she died of embolism if she hadn't been buried.

"Someone is running scared right now that some little peccadillo in their past is coming into public notice, I'd say. They saw Rosario was going to throw a scare into her. They added to it. She croaked right there. Now they're really up shit's creek! Whatever she had on them is going to come out!"

"You said it's a big 'So what?'"

"They don't know that. Yet.

"Tonio, if we just tell people about what we did when we were teenagers it would take away anyone's ability to do this crap to us. We'd even probably find everyone else did things they're worried about. That's what a lot of women do. They tell their best friend a secret in trade of a secret from the friend. They get to giggling about how silly it was and the fear and such is gone.

"I saw that demonstrated by Dave – you met him. My weird writer friend – when somebody saw him hugging an Indio on the dock at Chiriqui Grande. It's just the way the Indios are. They touch and hug. It's not more than that, but this couple of gringo women there said, 'Get a room!'

"Dave grinned at them and said to take a good look at Andres. They'd be damned jealous of him if he did get a room. He'd done it before and probably would again. When he was in the rock bands in the late sixties there was a song, *Love the One You're With,* that they took too far, sometimes.

"They all started laughing then. The women agreed they *would* be jealous. Andres is one hell of a handsome man!

"If Dave had been laid by a guy or two when he was in the hippie music scene and tried to hide it he would have reacted in a very different way. He said that he'd been laid before and sort of enjoyed it. Show him thirty guys his age and twenty had been laid by a guy before. Big fucking deal! It happens to a lot of people."

"So now they get whatever she died for released anyhow and no one cares. I see what you mean. They've been running scared for years because of something that has no meaning to anyone else.

That could make them want revenge on others for lesser reasons.

"Well, we can go see Joyce now. Doc called and said she's awake and coherent."

"Let's see if she can shed a little light on this one," Clint agreed.

"Your entry into cliche of the month?"

That got him the finger.

They got to the hospital and were shown in. Lloyd and Hank were there, but the officer at her door wouldn't let anyone except the doctor and one nurse in. Joyce had some bandages and was bruised, but would recover fully. They chatted a bit about what had happened.

"Tell us what happened from the time when you started the trek until you woke up here," Tonio suggested. "Take your time. Don't leave anything out."

"Well, we started at that little shed thing. There were two backpackers from Germany and two from France who were together. Ilene and I were the only other two. The man there told us some safety rules and said he was an official guide, but we would have to pay for him to go with us.

"Ilene said we knew how to walk a trail, so no thanks. The backpackers had done lots of trails in several countries. They didn't need help either.

"They left about five minutes before we did. Ilene couldn't decide what she wanted to take so we just took some food and bottled water and our cameras – where is my camera?"

"We have it," Tonio replied.

"Oh, good! It *is* beautiful up there!

"Well, we finally got started. Ilene actually said she liked that kind of thing and she was glad we came. When we came to places where you can look out over a valley it could take your breath away!

"We were going slow. I had figured we could reach the Boquete end in seven hours going slow. We wouldn't miss anything

"We got to just past where you go under those really tall trees, they call them nispero, when someone really close behind called to us to wait up. We stopped and waited. It was maybe ten feet past that sharp bend with the big boulder sticking out the side of the mountain.

"Everything suddenly went black. Somebody put a sack or cloth of some sort over my head. It was a man. He said to stay quiet and we wouldn't be hurt. Ilene seemed to think this was somebody who knew who she was and wanted to get a big ransom. I thought it was some silly publicity thing she'd thought up to sell more books.

"I was being pushed along back toward where we came from. I tripped and the man who was behind me yanked me up and said to not play games or he'd knock me out and carry me. He shoved me and I went down. Ilene was really getting scared the way she sounded like this wasn't supposed to be what was happening. One man said she needed a lesson in respect.

"I got really scared then. I was laying there and I remembered what she did with those gangsters at the restaurant and thought they were going to do something horrible. Maybe rape us to teach us a lesson.

"I had a rock by my hand and hit the man who was trying to yank me to my feet and ran. I pulled the sack off my head and went around the bend and remembered too late how sharp the turn was and that there was nothing on the outer side of the trail but a little ledge. I fell over the ledge and woke up here.

"The doctor says that they found Ilene. From what he wouldn't say ... she's dead?"

"Yes, I'm afraid so," Tonio answered. "Did you know she had a brain embolism?"

"Embolism? She had headaches sometimes. The doctor said there was a little shadow, but it wasn't the kind of thing from cancer or anything. It might be something that put pressure on a spot in her brain. He said a lot of people had that kind of thing and that he personally thought they'd find it in all the people who got migraines. The X-ray didn't show it up very well and we couldn't afford an MRI scan."

"It seems her experience was so frightening that the embolism ruptured and killed her," Tonio said. "We would have to file it as natural causes with mitigating circumstances. If someone hadn't buried her there we wouldn't have been able to prosecute. Doing that showed us the death was planned, if not in the way it happened."

"It did?" Hank asked.

"A person doesn't often take a shovel along on a mountain trail hike," Tonio replied. There wasn't any reply to that.

"Okay. We've gotten a pretty clear picture of things," Clint said. "What did she have she could blackmail you with?"

There was a shocked dead silence for a few seconds from her, Lloyd and Hank.

"I ... she had ... it was a long time ago ... it was mostly just ... embarrassing. I had it pretty good with her paying for everything so I acted like it was a big thing.

"I had a ... an affair. With a woman. She had pictures."

"You actually wrote her books?"

"I ... she came up with the story and some of the things, the sexy parts. I put them into a more readable format. She really didn't have any talent for writing. Hank is good with words whenever I got in a rut. Those romance things are just plain silly to me. He thinks the same, but it was fun for him. Not for me. I was serious. I knew it was a way to make a lot of money. I'd never had much. When Dad died I got scared I couldn't make a living myself. That's when I had the affair. A woman who owned a business. That was why I had a job. Mom died last year and Ilene showed me her diary. I read it and said it would make a good romance novel if she would take the overdone descriptions out.

"She said it was all true. She'd done all that. Some of it was really kinky.

"I told her that wasn't the way to present it. Licking his balls and then doing a sixty nine, then he screwed her in the ass was telling too much. Tell the start and let people's imagination fill in the gaps.

"She was damned good at that! It's why the crap sold. She could claim that she was against pornography, but was for good clean sex between adults and come off as a decent person instead of what she was. A sick pervert!

"She worked with me and we had the first book. It sold a little. She went looking for an agent and came up with Lloyd. He handled the second book that sold about like the first. It brought in a few dollars, but not enough to live on.

"We got Hank to help. He's good at what he calls continuity. We didn't have that in the first two. He said they were just jerky stop and start reading, but the stories were good. Certain things were better than good.

"We wrote the third one, and it took off right away. Hank and I went back and used the same formula on the first two. Rhey started selling, too.

"Ilene let it go to her head. She started thinking she was a famous author now and wanted to be treated like a famous person. She wanted to do the talk show circuit and star in a movie taken from one of her books.

"She had no talent. It would be disaster.

"Lloyd and Hank suggested that we actually go to the places she used in her books. We could then claim part of it was taken from reality. The people who read those things want to believe things can actually happen like that.

"I mean, here's this super-stud handsome macho ladykiller lover who lays twenty women in the first five pages and he falls hopelessly in love with a silly empty-headed virgin who treats him like leftover pig slop?

"Anyhow, it worked. Here we are. It doesn't seem to have the happy ending where she runs off into the jungle with super-stud to live ecstatically ever after."

"That about it for you, Lloyd? She got you into a kinky relationship and filmed things?" Clint asked.

"Seeing it will all come out anyhow, more or less. The books at first weren't much, but she could cause me to lose my license just when things were starting to happen. I worked extra hard on the third one because it had everything for that market. They buy on strict formula. The most important part of the formula is the sex scenes. If they're believable and erotic, even pornographic, the book has a decent chance of being published. If they're erotic without being pornographic they can be published. The author goes on that talk show circuit, then I've got it made. This one had that.

"She does have an offer for making a movie from it, but there's no way in hell she could be in it at all, much less as the star. She couldn't act her way out of a wet paper bag with the bottom torn out. She was getting next to impossible about it. If she couldn't star, there would be no movie rights.

"Do you know how much they pay for a book they make into a movie? Two point five million dollars! She wouldn't have to lift a finger the rest of her life! I would have an in into Hollywood and could have a list of clients that I can only dream about without it!"

"So you killed her and can now sell the movie rights?" Tonio asked.

"No! I could talk her into it! I was planning to have her publisher tell me, in a certified letter, that her book would be withdrawn from the market. They had the exclusive printing rights and would drop her if she didn't allow the great publicity that would be gained from having it made into a movie.

"They couldn't do that, of course. She didn't know that. She would see her fame disappearing and would consent. I would then have a contract drawn up with the studio that said she could be listed as a co-director, which would make her a star when it became the bestselling movie of the year!

"She would dream of that and would have gone along with anything."

"But she had that blackmail evidence. What then?" Clint asked.

"Nothing then. I would make it plain that she got rid of it and that I got a signed affidavit that she had made it up.

"You see, my contract with her ... I don't have one. You can see this puts me in a very bad spot. If Joyce doesn't give me one, I'm out.

"I will see that the book suddenly stops selling and that she never gets anything else published.

"Joyce, it will change nothing except that I'll have a legal contract for what I've done and will do."

"You made it work. I always thought you had a contract. You can certainly continue with it. I'll certainly give you a binding contract. Fair is fair."

"So that leaves Hank," Tonio said. "What's your story?"

"I don't know. She said she had some things that would cause me trouble, but I don't think she had. She tried to set me up a couple of times, but I saw what was happening. I didn't tumble.

"I'm just a paid consultant. I had the upper hand in a way because I could tell the world she didn't actually write anything. She only came up with a story line that Joyce and I wrote.

"I've learned to avoid her in her worst periods. We got along, if in a sort of lukewarm way."

"She didn't hold the gay thing over your head?" Clint asked.

"It's bi, but no. If you know it, how could she blackmail me?"

"You have a point," Clint replied.

Clint and Tonio finished the interview and went back to the station. Something more would have to come up or this would never go anywhere. He can still lose his license so a contract with Joyce won't mean much," Tonio suggested.

"I think Joyce would come forward and tell them, and it would probably be true, that Ilene intentionally set him up for that. It was by mutual consent so has no legal standing."

"Don't take my arguments away from me!"

"Better me than in a court where some lawyer would point it out."

"Hank? There's something phony about him, but there's something phony about all of them."

"They're in a phony situation where the book's author was phony the scenario was phony the action was phony and the promotion was phony, at best. Joyce may be the only one who's not phony, but I felt she was holding something back there."

"They were all holding something back."

"That's what makes it so difficult."

They discussed everything and decided to see what actually came out. If it matched what they'd been told it would mean there was something else behind the death.

"*Death of a Bitch*. That was a story Dave wrote in Florida. That's what we have here."

"Oh, good! Dave wrote the solution to this one in Florida fifteen years ago!"

"Except she died from cyanide in a candy bar or something and it was thirty years ago." That got him the finger.

They didn't think they could get more unless something happened or there was something from the blackmail – if that ever showed up.

The phone rang. It was for Tonio. He put it on speaker.

"Yes?"

"Officer Valdez? Antonio Valdez?"

"Yes."

"I'm Lawrence Samuel Davidson, attorney for the late Ilene Carstairs. I was instructed to contact you by her sister, Miss Joyce Carstairs. I am instructed that I may tell you what Miss Carstairs left with me to release in the event of her death.

"Officer Valdez, it is blackmail evidence. I did not know this until ten minutes ago. It will not be released. It will be – has already been, in fact, as of two minutes ago – destroyed. I will be no party to blackmail!

"I am to tell you that the evidence held is very like what was told to you in Chiriqui Hospital by the persons involved. As that is a true statement so long as Mr. Henry Little, Mr. Lloyd Baskins and Miss Joyce Carstairs are concerned. There is other evidence against nine other people who will be informed the evidence no longer exists.

"If there are further questions, I will attempt to answer them so long as it does not breach the confidence of the persons.... What I'm saying is that I ain't about to tell you what was in that evidence beyond a very limited point."

"Good enough. You can confirm what we were told. Lloyd was filmed or video-recorded in kinky sex acts with Ilene?"

"Affirmative."

"Joyce was video-recorded or filmed in lesbian acts?"

"Affirmative."

"Little was ... wasn't filmed, was he?"

"No. He was involved in some things that concerned minors. I am somewhat torn about his case. Minors become a different thing. I'll say alcohol was involved. Joyce informed me you probably knew about some of that."

"Yes. From the time he was also a minor. I'll just ask the age of the youngest?

"Mr. Davidson, a minor on the comarca where I live most of the time is fourteen years old in my estimation, but twelve, legally."

"There is no instance of anyone nearly that young involved in anything. I don't see how a fourteen year old can be considered old enough not to be badly affected by these things."

"It's a very different culture. We don't make the child feel guilty because of things that happen where they have no control. The kids grow up knowing that any number of things might happen, that people are individuals. I'm not talking about what they may be forced to do. That's considered a violation of a person and is dealt with very harshly, regardless of age."

"I can accept that intellectually. I'm not sure I can emotionally."

"It's the way you were raised. I was raised in the states. I can see what happens from the psychological angle when you're raised with the idea that anything that happens to you in certain areas is *wrong* and that *you* are responsible somehow for causing those things to happen. When something does happen the kid carries a guilt complex the rest of his life. Here, he knows that those things *do* happen and that he's not guilty of anything.

"I can't explain it. It's like my son said in a restaurant here. The city children don't have a place. They spend their lives looking for a place to belong."

Davidson laughed. "So your son is a teenager and knows anything that happened to him isn't his fault."

"No, Clint's son is two years old and knows about life," Tonio answered. "The Indios will surprise hell out of you by what they know at two years old."

There was a silence. "Two years old and that ... wise?"

"We Indios will surprise you. Thanks for the information. I think you just made a difficult case impossible."

They soon rang off. Tonio looked at Clint and shrugged. He asked if Clint would go back to his family in the morning.

"I suppose so. If nothing else happens, we're pissing up a rope with this one."

Tonio nodded.

"Clint? Get over here! I'm at Chiriqui! Joyce was attacked!" Tonio demanded over the phone. Clint looked at the clock. 2:57 AM.

"Attacked? Is she hurt?"

"No. Get over here! This one will be solved in no time. Attacking Joyce was a grave mistake made by someone who had gotten away with murder if he hadn't tried this stupidity!"

"On my way!"

He jumped up and slipped into his clothes and headed out. He wasn't far from the hospital, which was fortunate. There were no taxis around at that hour. He arrived at the hospital and went directly to Joyce's room where Tonio and a female officer were talking with Joyce.

"Okay! I'm here! What happened?"

"Miss Carstairs was awakened when a man came into the room through the ceiling (she pointed to where a panel from the drop ceiling was slid aside). She ran into the bath and locked the door. He opened the door with a pocket knife or screwdriver or something," the female officer, Gloria, said. "She can tell you the rest."

"It was horrible! He dropped down and came toward me. I ran into the bath and locked the door, but he opened it. I could hear him trying to force the lock, then knew he could come right in because they only lock so people will know if they're occupied. Anything will open them.

"I didn't know what to do! There was no way out!

"I thought about ten thousand plans, none of which could possibly work. I did know how hair spray will blind you for a couple of minutes if you get it in your eyes. I had a can, so I could try to blind him and get by. I also knew he would have to move back or I *couldn't* get by!

"I saw a thing on TV a year or so ago about dangerous things in the house. Hair spray was one of them! In a pressure can the spray burns like a flamethrower! I had a cigarette lighter!

"As soon as the door opened I lit the lighter and aimed it for his head. I sprayed. He screamed and ran. His hair was on fire! I saw that! It was very black hair. Long.

"Anyhow, he got out somehow. Maybe through the ceiling or something. I had slammed the door and locked it again.

"I waited a minute. I thought the scream would bring someone, but no one came. I went out in the hall, but there was no one there.

"I came back in a pushed the call button. Here you are."

"There was an emergency call from the entrance and the night nurse was there. It was a false alarm," Tonio said.

"So! We're looking for someone whose hair is burned off and who has probably gotten some serious facial burns," Clint said. "There can't be many running around this time of night."

"Was he wearing gloves?" Tonio asked.

"I don't know. He had a mask across his face. Like a towel wrapped around like those terrorists have?"

Tonio picked up a knife from under the bed with his handkerchief. "I suppose he had gloves. I think maybe he left this little item behind.

"I'm sorry, Miss Carstairs. I thought the danger to you was past. This means you know something that is still deadly to a murderer.

"Gloria, please have Little and Baskins picked up immediately." She nodded and went out.

"I think it would be wise to have you assigned another room," Tonio said to Joyce, who nodded.

"What did you neglect to tell us that someone feels is dangerous to him?" Clint asked.

"I don't really know! I'm scared!"

"You have every right to be," Tonio replied. "Let's get you into a more secure room. If anyone tells anyone else which room, for any reason, they'll be the ones who better get scared."

They went out into the hall where Tonio gave instructions to the night nurse. She took Joyce to another room. She wasn't even to let Clint and Tonio know which one it was.

Clint and Tonio went to the station to wait for Baskins and Little to be brought in.

Neither was in his room. Clint thought a minute and said to check La Esmeralda. Gloria grinned and gave him a thumbs up.

"Motive, considering that they were both off the hook?" Tonio asked.

Clint thought. "Baskins will be at La Esmeralda and Little will be where we can find him soon enough."

"How do you figure?"

"He was wearing a towel. He screamed when his hair caught on fire, but it didn't get his eyes, directly, very much. His face won't have burns because of the towel. There probably wasn't much of his hair burned if any at all."

"A wig. We can spot that!"

"No we can't. It was a wig that got burned."

Tonio nodded and looked grim. "We can't let him get by with this!"

"Oh, we won't. He'll depend on macro and I'll be looking for micro."

"What in *hell* does that mean?"

"That would be telling!"

They went to a Pio Pio for coffee. They're open twenty four hours. Clint was used to fine coffee so considered this mud, and not very good quality mud.

When they went back to the station, Gloria had Lloyd there, waiting

"I asked Javier how long he'd been there. He said he was there since about nine thirty," Gloria reported. "There was no way he left in between."

"Put out a call to arrest Henry Little on a charge of attempted murder," Clint said. "I didn't need the report to know Lloyd didn't do it."

"How?" from Tonio.

"Micro." He got the finger.

Half an hour later an officer brought Little in. Clint took one look and said, "You're done! Book him and I can go home today."

"Yes. He was the only one who had the time," Tonio agreed.

"No. He can almost surely account for the time with only a little doubt.

"Where were you from two thirty until about three this morning, Mr. Little?"

"Clint? Mr. Little? What's going on?"

"Where were you and with whom, Mr. Little?" Tonio asked.

"I was with a ... with a man. Naldo Flores. We spent a little time, er, in bed."

"Well, he can confirm, of course?"

"Certainly!"

"He didn't perchance drop off to sleep for a short while? Ten minutes?" Clint asked.

"We both fell asleep for awhile."

"Micro! I see!" Tonio exploded. "Why have your eyebrows been painted on, Mr. Little?"

"Because my eyebrows are always painted on. The natural ones were removed. Electrolysis. Five years ago."

Tonio raised an eyebrow at Clint.

"Were your eyelashes also removed through electrolysis?" Clint asked. "Micro, Tonio. Brows are macro."

Tonio gave him the finger. Gloria laughed. She said she spotted that right away. After all, she's a woman and women see those things.

"Whatever. Book him," Tonio ordered.

"I want to speak with my lawyer! Now!" he demanded.

"Yeah, yeah. Tomorrow," Gloria said. "Come on. I'm supposed to be off shift for more than an hour."

He looked totally confused as she led him out.

"What the hell happened here?!" Lloyd cried.

"Someone tried to kill Joyce. She lit a fire on his head. His eyelashes were burned off. It was you or Hank. You still have your eyelashes," Clint said. "It's too late to go back to bed. Let's get some breakfast."

Clint swung Nito around as he got off the helicopter. Tyna came out to hug them both. The chopper took off. They went inside where Clint got out of the clothes he'd worn for two days. He headed for the shower he'd designed where the whole family played in the water awhile. Tyna went to fix something for breakfast. Nito sat on Clint's lap and hugged him. He nuzzled his lips into Nito's thick black hair.

He was home. Back in paradise.

After a delicious breakfast Clint went to the garden Nito took great pride in keeping. Nito explained that there were too many bugs when he got back from David, but they were under control now. The cow was pregnant. Ernesto had come by with four kinds of frijoles and a lot of corn. It was mostly dried corn that he and Tyna had ground. They would have plenty of corn meal for tortillas or corn bread. Tyna made some avena mix.

The family walked along the river a distance to the swimming hole. There were several children and youths playing in the water. They joined them. They liked to wrestle with Clint in the water.

After awhile they went back to the house where Clint laid around for the afternoon doing next to nothing. Tomorrow he would go with Bino to cut nispero all day. Nito would go fishing with Omar.

About five thirty his cell phone buzzed. He answered. It was Tonio.

"Clint? Just a report. We have the whole story from Little. It's sort of sordid. Joyce and Lloyd are going back to the states tomorrow. It seems Joyce does have some talent and Lloyd thinks she can be a part of the movie if not the star.

"You'll want to know from when Ilene was killed. I'll read the report the way it's filed:

I was supposed to jump out and take Ilene away to hide when Joyce wasn't close. They were not far past where I was waiting when two men I've seen in David somewhere came to throw sacks over their heads. I thought probably Lloyd had come up with the same idea, so I could stay out of it. I didn't think it would be such a great idea. That sort of thing went out in the fifties. I only agreed because Ilene was blackmailing me.

Anyhow, Joyce came running back a ways down the trail and I kept going. Maybe it was the plan that she would escape to report Ilene had been abducted, or something such. Joyce wouldn't know a thing about it, because she wouldn't go that far.

I followed them to near that stream. They were a little rough with her, but not serious or bad. They showed her some pictures. They went away and she was sitting there on a rock, scared to death!

I had a shovel with me because I was to drop it somewhere so they would look for a grave. That was Ilene's idea. She would show up in a couple of days with a story of how clever she had been to escape.

She could never have pulled it off. She can't act. She can't begin to act!

Anyhow, she was on that rock and was mad as hell at me for not rescuing her when they grabbed her. I said I thought it was just another plan and that Lloyd had set it up.

She said she was going to show me how smart it was to let them treat her that way! She was going to tell the world about me! She was going to show the world the pictures she had!

I tried to reason with her. It's was never even possible when she was in her bitch mood. She couldn't understand why I would let two big professional hoods treat her like a common hag!

I said, "My god, Ilene! Look at me! How in hell could I do anything with two professional hoods who were both twice my size?"

She said she was going to expose me for the prissy little coward I was.

I said I'd really kill her then. The only reason I hadn't already was only because she had those pictures. If they were going to get out, anyhow, there was no reason to not.

She stood up and said she could beat my ass herself, and she was a woman. She came at me and I knocked her down. She started to get up and I said I'd kick her ugly face until she wouldn't be able to show it in public the rest of her life. She started to get up and I drew my foot back. I was pissed enough then that I was considering actually kicking her in the face.

She sort of gurgled and fell down. I waited for her to feel she had calmed me down, but she never moved. I checked and she had no pulse.

I was scared out of my mind, almost. She was dead and I didn't know why. I knew they would blame me, if they found me there.

I had the shovel. I dug on a sandbar and put her in the hole and covered her, then got out and came back to David.

It looked like it would be alright. I talked with you cops and said that she was probably going to show something she had set up that was false photography or something. It was going to work out. Lloyd and Joyce told their stories and I threw mine in. Joyce had the lawyer who had the stuff get rid of it. I didn't know until then that he would never have released blackmail evidence. He hadn't even known that's what it was until Joyce told him to get rid of it and to call you and tell you what we said was true. In the hospital, you know.

Joyce stopped me on the way out and said there wouldn't ever be anything said about what I was being blackmailed about, so long as I didn't ever do anything like that again. She would see that it did come out if she ever heard I'd been with a minor again.

I had been. Here. With two. They were fourteen and fifteen. Two really handsome Indian kids. I thought they were offering me ... to go with me. I couldn't resist.

I never in my life initiated anything with a minor. Never! I only did what they wanted.

I swear, I didn't try to get them to do anything. They told me they wanted to try some things and I could ... like I did things to them they asked. They didn't have to do anything at all. They had a good time and we did it again the next day. Two days ago.

They had to go back to the comarca and thanked me for ... for showing them so much fun.

I knew Joyce would find out about it. She always seemed to know things. She wouldn't do any blackmail, but she would turn me in. My life would be ruined.

I went crazy. I made a plan to kill her. You know what happened.

I heard that the Indio kids were not minors anymore when they were fourteen and that I wouldn't even get in trouble if they didn't do anything, only me. Is that true? Did I get in this mess when I didn't have to? When I was home free?

"Did he? Do it for nothing?"

"If he only did what they wanted, probably. The parents wouldn't think anything of it. The kids know about a lot of it and want to see what it's like at that age. Sex is always fun if you're doing it because you want to. Big deal!"

"I guess. It's not how I was raised. At least this one's over at last. I didn't really think we'd ever know for awhile there."

"It was too possible a lot of the time. He was right that he'd have been home free if he hadn't gone after Joyce."

"What does she have to say about it?"

"Nothing. We showed her the report and she said maybe this would teach him a lesson. He hadn't really done anything that bad except to try to kill her. That didn't work. He got the dirty end of the stick on that.

"We don't have anything without her testimony, Clint. What do you think?"

"I said it had to be solved. We solved it. I don't care past that. It's another case where letting him go home with the fact that he'll be listed as undesirable here saves Panamá the price of housing and feeding him for the next five or ten years."

"I have to agree. How's the family?"

C. D. Moulton's works are available on most major outlets as printed or e-books. CD writes the CD Grimes, PI, mysteries, the Det. Lt. Nick Storie mysteries, the Clint Faraday mysteries, the Flight of the Maita science fiction series, books on orchid culture and many others of many types. Mystery, adventure, intrigue, science fiction, humor, fantasy, paranormal, mild erotica, and factual.